Look for more books
in the GOOSEBUMPS PRESENTS series:

Episode #2 *The Cuckoo Clock of Doom*

Goosebumps®

PRESENTS

THE GIRL WHO CRIED MONSTER

Adapted by Megan Stine
From the teleplay by Charles Lazer
Based on the novel by R.L. Stine

SCHOLASTIC INC.
New York Toronto London Auckland Sydney

A PARACHUTE PRESS BOOK

No part of this publication may be reproduced in whole or in part, or stored in a retrieval system, or transmitted in any form or by any means, electronic, mechanical, photocopying, recording, or otherwise, without written permission of the publisher. For information regarding permission, write to Scholastic Inc., 555 Broadway, New York, NY 10012.

ISBN 0-590-74586-7

12 11 10 9 8 7 6 5 4 3 2 1   6 7 8 9/9 0 1/0
40

Printed in the U.S.A.

First Scholastic printing, March 1996

THE GIRL WHO CRIED MONSTER

1

"Lucy!" My little brother called to me from the other side of the yard. "I can't reach my ball! It's way in the bushes."

It was a lazy summer afternoon. My brother, Randy, and I were hanging around in our backyard. Our dog was asleep near the big tree.

My name is Lucy Dark. I'm twelve years old. My brother is six. He has dark brown hair and brown eyes like me. But he's just a little kid, so he always wants me to help him with something.

"Lucy — aren't you going to come?" Randy whined.

I wiggled my bare feet in the grass. It felt nice not to wear shoes.

Then I looked over at Randy. He was standing near the bushes. With his bare foot, he was trying to reach the ball.

I ran over and stood beside Randy.

"Randy! Get away from there!" I cried. "Don't you know what's under there?"

I opened my eyes wide and watched the bushes carefully.

"No. What?" Randy whispered. He edged closer to me.

"The Toe-biter," I said calmly.

Randy gulped. Then he glanced back at the bushes. "What's a Toe-biter?" he asked. I saw him curl up his toes to try to hide them.

"You know," I answered. "It's just what it sounds like. A *Toe-biter*. Chomp! Chomp! Chomp!"

Randy tried to look brave. "So what?" he said. "If it's a monster, it can't get us now. Monsters only come out at night."

"Not true," I replied. "The Toe-biter isn't a night monster. It bites anytime."

Randy watched the bushes carefully. The wind blew. The leaves moved. The bushes seemed to be alive.

He pulled his toes back even more.

Ha, ha, I thought. *He is really scared. He is afraid the Toe-biter will get him.*

I picked up a stick and poked at the ball in the bushes.

"It got Becky and Lilah next door," I told Randy.

"When?" Randy asked. He looked upset.

"When they were playing in their wading pool," I said.

Randy's eyes grew big. "Couldn't they see it coming?" he asked.

"No." I shook my head. "The Toe-biter can change shapes. It can make itself look like *anything.* Like grass . . . dirt . . . even water."

"What happened?" Randy asked.

I grabbed Randy's hand and pulled him close.

"First Becky felt a tickle," I told him. "She thought it was the dog licking her toes. But the dog wasn't even there. Then the tickling started to hurt. It felt like something chewing on both of her feet. With sharp, pointy little teeth. Becky pulled her feet away, but it was too late. All her toes were gone!"

"You're lying," Randy said.

"No, I'm not," I said. "Ask Becky. Ask her to take off her shoes. She'll show you. Ask her."

I poked around in the bushes a few more times. I couldn't reach the ball, so I threw down the stick and stepped closer. I stuck my bare foot into the bushes, toward the ball.

"Don't use your foot!" Randy cried. He grabbed my arm and tried to pull me back.

"I'll do it real quick," I said as I reached farther under with my foot.

Randy watched me, still gripping my arm. He bit his lip.

"Be careful . . . " he moaned.

Out of the corner of my eye, I could see him watching the grass. And the bushes. Every time the wind blew, he gripped my arm harder.

All of a sudden, my leg shot forward. As if something were pulling on it.

"Aaahh!" I screamed. "Ow! Ow!"

"What?" Randy cried in his high, babyish voice.

"It hurts!" I yelled. "It hurts!"

"*What* hurts?" Randy screamed.

"Aaaahhh! Get it off me!" I cried.

I yanked my foot out from under the bushes as fast as I could. With a gasp, I stared down at my bare foot. Randy looked down, too.

All the toes on my left foot were missing!

Randy let out a scream like I've never heard before in my life.

"Aaaaahhh!" he cried. "Your toes! They're gone!"

2

"Aahh! The Toe-biter got me!" I cried.

Randy screamed and took off running. He ran to the house as fast as his chubby little legs would carry him.

He pushed open the kitchen door.

"Mom!" I heard him yell. "Come quick! The Toe-biter got Lucy!"

Then I heard my mom's voice.

"Randy," she said with a sigh. "You know there's no such thing as a Toe-biter."

"Yes, there is! Her toes are all gone!" Randy cried.

I laughed and reached under the bushes. Randy's ball was wedged under a branch. I yanked it out.

Then I skipped across the grass. I tossed my long brown hair behind my shoulders and pranced into the house.

"Ha, ha," I said. I gave my little brother a smirky smile.

Randy stared down at my bare feet. All of my toes were fine. All ten of them.

"Lucy, would you *please* stop scaring your brother," my mom said. She rolled her eyes.

"Oh, Mom, it was just a *joke*," I told her. "Randy is such a baby. He will believe anything."

Randy was still staring at my feet. "How did your toes grow back?" he asked.

"Well . . ." I started.

For a minute, I thought about telling him the truth. That I had rolled my toes under my foot. That I made it look like they were gone.

But I didn't tell him the truth. I smiled instead. "Well," I told Randy, "the Toe-biter gave my toes back to me. If I promised to let him take yours — tonight!"

"Lucy!" my mom snapped. "Stop that right now!"

She gave me one of her squinty stares. "What about your Summer Reading project?" she asked. "You haven't been to the library for a couple of days. Go bother Mr. Mortman for a while."

Good idea, I thought. I love the library — even if it is a scary-looking place.

I grabbed my backpack and Rollerblades. I hurried out of the house and sat down on the front steps. I was going to put on my Rollerblades.

Then I remembered. It wasn't worth putting them on. No Rollerblades were allowed in the library. I decided to walk. It was only eight blocks. Then I would Rollerblade on the way home.

It was late afternoon when I got to the library. The sky was sort of spooky gray. The library looked scary as usual.

The library is in an old house. The outside is dark wood. The roof is pointy. There are two weird towers that look like spikes. Big trees grow all around the building. It's always shady.

But so what? I thought. It's just a library. I love all the books inside.

Still, when I reached the steps of the library, something told me not to go in. But I didn't listen.

Mr. Mortman, the librarian, was busy when I entered the main room. He was putting books on the shelves. And telling everyone to be quiet. He does that all the time.

Mr. Mortman is bald. And kind of fat. And he has beady black eyes. They looked tiny in the dark library. He was wearing a green turtleneck sweater that day.

"Hello, Lucy," he whispered as I walked past the front desk.

I nodded to him. I knew the rules. No talking, unless you had to.

I walked through the stacks of books, just to see if anyone I knew was there. My friend Aaron was sitting on the floor in the back. In the science-fiction section.

Aaron was busy reading, so I didn't bother him.

I walked back up to the front desk. Mr.

Mortman always liked to talk to me when I brought a book back. That was part of the Summer Reading program.

I plopped my book down on the counter, in front of Mr. Mortman. He looked especially creepy that day.

"So, what did you think of it?" he asked me in a very quiet voice.

I glanced at the book — a story about a horse. *Black Beauty*.

"Two thumbs down," I announced. I wrinkled up my nose. "It was boring."

"But Lucy, *Black Beauty* is a classic," Mr. Mortman said.

"It would have been better if the horse had two heads," I said. "And maybe some big fangs."

Mr. Mortman sort of smiled. He pointed to a cart full of Summer Reading books.

"Why don't you pick out another book?" he said, very softly.

I nodded and walked over to the cart. Hmmm, I thought. Maybe I can find something scary. Something with a monster in it.

While I was looking through the books, Aaron came up. He's my age, but he's taller than I am. He has curly black hair and is really skinny.

"Hey, Lucy, what are you getting?" Aaron asked.

I snatched a book from the pile and showed it to him.

"*Frankenstein*," I announced with a big smile.

Mr. Mortman smiled, too. "Are you sure, Lucy?" he asked me. "*Frankenstein* is a classic, too. Just like *Black Beauty*."

"Yeah, but it's got a monster," I said.

"Wouldn't it be cool if there were real monsters?" Aaron said.

"I don't think everyone would agree with you," Mr. Mortman said. He stamped my book to check it out. "Most people like to get scared in movies or stories. But *not* in real life."

Mr. Mortman stared at me when he said that. Like he was asking me a question. But I didn't know what the question was — or the answer.

It was almost time for the library to close. So Aaron checked his book out, too. Then we left.

We started to walk home together. We talked about Mr. Mortman on the way. We named all the things we didn't like about him. His sweaty little hands. His beady eyes. His squeaky voice.

I thought Mr. Mortman was creepy. Aaron thought so, too.

Halfway home, I remembered something.

"Oh, no! My Rollerblades!" I said. "I left them at the library!"

"I'm sorry, but I can't go back with you," Aaron said. "I've got to get home."

"That's okay," I told him.

I turned and hurried back toward the library. It was almost dusk. The sun was sinking quickly.

I just hope the building isn't closed, I thought. I glanced up at the towers. They looked even spookier than before.

Why did I leave my stupid Rollerblades in

there? I thought. I didn't like the library at night.

I had reached the front steps. I put my foot on the first library step.

Something creaked.

My heart started to pound. Did a light inside the library just go out?

I took another step. It creaked, too.

I don't want to go in, I thought. I stood still.

All at once, I heard a branch crack.

Then something jumped at me. And I screamed.

3

"Merrrowww!"

A horrible screeching filled my ears. I stumbled back down the steps.

"Get off me!" I yelled. Then I saw a black cat running away. The cat had jumped on me from a big tree branch that hung over the library steps.

I took a deep breath and let it out. Phew! It was only a cat.

My heart was still beating fast. I walked up the steps again and opened the library door.

Inside, the air was cool and dark. Very dark. All the lights were out except one. It glowed in an office at the far end of the library.

It's too dark in here, I thought.

The silence was so creepy, I wanted to run. My footsteps echoed on the tile floor.

Hurry up, Lucy, I told myself. Find your Rollerblades and get out!

On tiptoe, I hurried to the main desk. I looked under a reading table nearby.

But my Rollerblades weren't there.

Where did I leave them? I wondered. I closed my eyes and thought hard, trying to remember. Think fast, I told myself.

Oh, yeah. Suddenly I remembered. I had dropped them on a chair at a table near the door.

I hurried to the table. There they were. I grabbed my Rollerblades and started to leave.

But something stopped me.

Was someone humming?

"Hmmm-da-deee-da-dum." A voice sang softly in the distance.

I whirled around. I stared at the light glowing in the back of the library. It gave off a creepy glow.

I listened hard.

"Ooh, it's time now," a voice said. The voice was high and squeaky. It was Mr. Mortman. "It's time, my plump little beauties. You've been so good. I almost hate to do this . . ."

Do what? I was scared, but I wanted to know. I tiptoed toward Mr. Mortman's office.

There was a window in the wall of the office. I tiptoed some more.

When I was close enough, I saw him through the window. Mr. Mortman was alone near his desk. The desk lamp made huge, wild shadows on the wall.

Then I saw the jars on Mr. Mortman's desk. They were filled with live, hopping crickets.

There was a cage on his desk, too. It contained two or three huge black spiders. Tarantulas!

I was super quiet. I held my breath and watched. I hoped Mr. Mortman wouldn't see me.

"Don't be shy," Mr. Mortman said. He reached for the jar of crickets. "It's dinnertime."

His sweaty hand unscrewed the jar lid. I thought I heard the crickets start to chirp.

What's he doing? I wondered. The crickets are going to get out!

But they didn't escape. Mr. Mortman quickly shoved his hand into the jar. He pulled out a fistful of crickets.

For a minute, he held the crickets over the tarantula cage.

What's he waiting for? I wondered. Why doesn't he drop the crickets in?

All at once, I gasped.

In the lamplight, I could see Mr. Mortman's face changing shape!

At first, it just grew bigger. And bigger. Then his whole head floated up out of his turtleneck sweater. Like a turtle, poking his head out of his shell.

An instant later, Mr. Mortman grew ugly. His eyes bulged out. They turned huge and slimy. They grew so big, they looked like giant doorknobs. And they bobbed on long stems.

His skin was terrible, too. Dry and crusty, like one big scab.

I wanted to scream. But I didn't. I kept quiet, so Mr. Mortman wouldn't know I was there.

All at once, he opened his mouth. It wasn't a human mouth. It was a big black hole.

He jammed the fistful of crickets into his mouth-hole. Then he started chewing them.

"NO!" I screamed silently. I couldn't believe it.

Mr. Mortman was a monster!

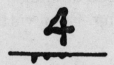

My arms and legs began to tremble.

I looked at the wall behind Mr. Mortman. There was a horrible shadow. A shadow of the Mortman Monster. It was big enough to eat me in one bite.

I finally opened my mouth to scream out loud. But nothing came out. I was too scared even to scream.

For a minute, I watched him chewing the crickets. The crunching made me sick. I wanted him to spit them out. It was grosser than gross.

I closed my eyes tight. If I don't look, maybe he will go away, I told myself.

But when I opened my eyes, there he was. Again.

He put his fist into the jar. Then he jammed another handful of crickets into his mouth.

"Hmmm-da-deee-da-dum." Mr. Mortman was still humming. Even with his mouth full of crickets!

My heart thumped in my chest so loudly, I was afraid Mr. Mortman would hear it. I turned and ran. Ran all the way to the front of the library and out the door.

The sky was even darker than before. A fierce wind whipped the tree branches over my head. As I started down the steps, *BAM!* The library door slammed shut behind me.

Oh, no, I thought. He's following me!

I turned to check. My foot caught in a crack in the sidewalk. I tripped and fell on the hard cement.

"Ow!" I yelled.

I looked back at the library door. At least Mr. Mortman wasn't there. He hadn't followed me.

As fast as I could, I jumped up. My feet and legs pounded the sidewalk as I ran home. I ran the whole eight blocks. I felt like he was chasing me — even if he wasn't.

Out of breath, I burst in through the kitchen door.

"Whoa! Slow down!" my mother said. "What's the hurry?"

I could hardly talk.

"Mom! Dad! It's a monster!" I finally said.

My mother hardly looked up. She and my dad were making meatballs at the counter. They went right on rolling the raw meat between their hands.

"A monster? Where?" my little brother said.

"At the library!" I shrieked.

"Lucy, don't you say 'Hi' anymore when you come in?" my dad said.

"Hi, Dad," I said quickly. "There's a monster at the library!"

My parents still ignored me. But Randy didn't.

"What kind of monster?" he asked.

"A slimy, disgusting one that eats bugs!" I told him.

"Lucy, could you help us out here?" my dad said. He pointed at the meatballs.

I dropped my Rollerblades and backpack. They made a thud. "Listen to me!" I screamed. "Mr. Mortman's a monster!"

"He sure is funny-looking," my brother agreed.

"Oh, Lucy," my father said. "When are you going to get over this monster thing?"

I gazed at my parents with big, hopeful eyes. I wanted them to believe me. I wanted it so much. But they didn't.

"You're making the meatballs too big," my mom told my dad.

"I happen to like big meatballs," my dad replied.

Please, Mom, I thought. Please, Dad.

You have to believe me — you have to!

5

I called Aaron that night. I called from my room and told him the whole story. About Mr. Mortman. Or *Monster* Mortman. That was more like it.

"Now, wait," Aaron said. "Start from the beginning again. What happened? Are you saying Mortman *looked* like a monster? Or are you saying he really was a monster?"

I let out a big sigh.

"He *is* a monster!" I practically yelled into the phone. "He changed shape! Don't you get it? His head grew up out of his body. His eyes popped out. And he was eating crickets!"

Aaron was silent on the other end of the phone.

"I was lucky to get out of there alive," I went on. "I mean, you should have seen him, Aaron. He wasn't human. He could have eaten *me*. I know it."

More silence. I figured Aaron was really scared. Freaked out. Like I was.

"It's not fair," I told him. "*No* one believes me. No one! They think I'm making it up."

"Wow, I wonder why?" Aaron finally said.

I pounded my desk with my fist. "Don't *you* believe me, either?"

"Come on, Lucy," Aaron said. "It *is* pretty weird. How can Mortman be a monster?"

Aaron went on talking. I hardly listened. I made a face. As if I were trying to squeeze my mouth and nose and eyes together. I wished Aaron could see me. So he'd know how mad I was.

Then I looked around my room. I happened to see my camera on my bookcase.

That's it! I thought. I'll take a picture of Monster Mortman. Then everyone will have to believe me!

All I had to do was one thing. Get up the nerve to face Mr. Mortman again.

"Aaron, I've got it!" I shouted into the phone. "If you want proof, just wait. I'll get proof!"

I stayed up late that night reading my book. I read the whole next day, too. I wanted to finish *Frankenstein* so I could take it back to the library.

It was late afternoon by the time I put the book in my backpack. The camera was hidden in there, too. Then I walked to the library.

Why does the sky turn dark every time I come here? I wondered.

The library seemed spookier than ever. The spikes on the roof looked taller. The trees were thicker. The shadows were longer.

I tried to swallow, but I couldn't. My throat was closing up tight.

I opened the library door slowly. Everything looked gloomy inside. It was so dark, I couldn't see at first. The door creaked shut behind me.

Where is Mr. Mortman? I wondered. I peered down a row of bookshelves. No one.

I looked down another row. Mr. Mortman? Not there.

Was he hiding somewhere? Waiting to get me?

Suddenly I felt nervous. My heart started pounding. I walked down every row of books — but they were all empty!

The whole library was empty! No one was there.

Then I saw him. Mr. Mortman was sitting all by himself at a table in the back. His hands were folded on the table in front of him. And he had a terrible smile on his face.

He looked as if he'd been waiting for me.

"Hello, Lucy," Mr. Mortman said.

Uh, oh, I thought. I'm all alone in the library — with a monster!

ove to scare my little brother, Randy. He screamed really loud when I told him about the Toe-biter monster in the bushes.

"Lucy, would you please stop scaring your brother," my mom said. "Oh, Mom, it's just a joke," I told her.

Mom sent me to the library to check out a book. Mr. Mortman, the librarian, gives me the creeps.

As I walked home with my friend Aaron, I realized that I left my Rollerblades in the library.

The library was dark when I returned. Then I heard a noise—
a strange noise.

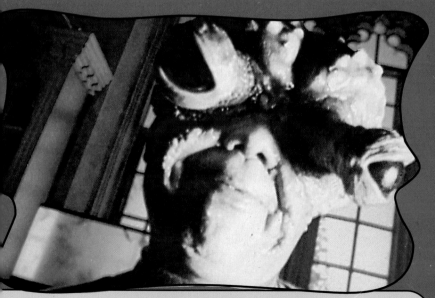

It was Mr. Mortman. He was turning into a huge, slimy, disgusting
monster!

"Mom! Dad! There's a monster in the library!" I cried when I ran into ou
kitchen. My parents didn't believe me.

The next night, I went back to the library to spy on Mr. Mortman.
"Dinnertime, my timid friend," Mr. Mortman said to a giant tarantula.

It was horrible. Mortman the Monster popped the tarantula right into his mouth! *CRUNCH. CRUNCH.*

I ran as fast as I could out of the library.

But when I made it home, the doorbell rang.
It was Mr. Mortman!

That night Mom and Dad invited Mr. Mortman to our house for dinner.
Randy and I were so scared.

Boy, was Mr. Mortman surprised when he found out what we were having for dinner—him!

But wait...now who is that horrible monster at our window?

6

A chill ran down my back. How come the library was so empty all of a sudden? Was I really all alone with Mr. Mortman?

I wanted to leave, too. But I had to stay. I had to get a picture of the monster.

Mr. Mortman called me to the table.

"Now, Lucy," he began. "Tell me how you liked this book."

"*Frankenstein*?" I said. My voice squeaked. It didn't sound like me. "Uh, it was good. Do you believe in monsters, Mr. Mortman?"

"I don't know about that," Mr. Mortman replied. "But I think we all have a little bit of a monster in us, don't you?"

I gulped. I know *you* do! I thought. Since you are one!

"Oh! Look at the time!" Mr. Mortman said, jumping up. "You'd better go choose another book. I'll tidy up. Everything must be put away."

Oh, sure, I thought. Let's clean up before dinnertime!

I picked out another book without even looking at it. I handed it to Mr. Mortman at the checkout desk.

"Hmmm," Mr. Mortman said, staring at the title. *"How to Fix Your Own TV.* Interesting choice."

Uh-oh. That's what I picked? I blushed.

"Uh, yeah," I said quickly. "I heard it's really good."

"Oh, really?" Mr. Mortman said. He raised one eyebrow. As if he didn't believe me. Finally he handed me the book. "I'll see you tomorrow, then?" he said.

"Uh, yeah. Right. See you," I said quickly.

Then I walked slowly to the front door.

But I didn't leave the library. I opened the

door and then slammed it shut instead — so Mr. Mortman would *think* I was gone.

The minute the door banged closed, all the lights in the library went out. All except one. The dim desk light in Mr. Mortman's office.

I crept forward on tiptoes. I inched across the library in the dark.

Everything seemed bigger with the lights out. The bookshelves seemed taller. The ceilings seemed higher.

I stubbed my toe on a book cart as I walked. But finally I reached my hiding place — behind a shelf of books near his office.

Mr. Mortman stood behind his desk, staring into the cage of tarantulas.

"Dinnertime, my timid friends," he said.

He reached for the jar of crickets.

I held my breath and watched as the horror started again. He began turning into a monster!

Don't run, I begged myself.

The truth was, I couldn't run. My legs were shaking too much. I had to stay there and watch.

I saw Mr. Mortman's head float up out of his collar. This time, his head grew almost twice as big as normal!

His eyes bulged out so much, I thought they might fall out. Then they began bobbling on their long stems.

I saw his mouth become a big, gaping black hole. Wider and darker than before.

Mr. Mortman picked up the jar of crickets and fumbled with it. It looked like he was hungry. But he was clumsy, too. He dropped the jar lid. All the crickets hopped out.

CHIRP! CHIRP-CHIRP! They hopped wildly from his desk to the floor.

Ha, ha, I thought. I hope you starve!

Mr. Mortman's tongue flicked out. Then he reached out and grabbed a cricket — just as it was jumping off his desk! He popped it into his mouth.

Uh-oh, I thought. If he sees me, I'm next!

I fumbled with the zipper on my backpack. I pulled out my camera and dropped the backpack on the floor. Then I glanced up at Mr. Mortman again. He was holding a tarantula up to his mouth.

"Dinnertime, my timid friend," Mr. Mortman said. "Mmmm — my favorite."

NO! Don't eat that tarantula! I wanted to scream. I covered my mouth so I wouldn't. But I had to watch. It was horrible. Mr. Mortman popped the tarantula right into his open jaw!

Mr. Mortman's cheeks bulged out. First one side and then the other.

The tarantula seemed to be running around in his ugly, black-hole mouth. Trying to escape!

Then one fuzzy black spider leg popped out of Mr. Mortman's mouth. It wiggled around.

Mr. Mortman picked up the leg between his fingers. Then he sucked it back into his mouth. It looked like he was sucking in a piece of spaghetti!

My heart pumped so fast, I felt as if I couldn't breathe.

But I knew what I had to do. I took a deep breath. Then I put the camera up to my eye and pressed the button.

Nothing happened. No click.

Dummy! I screamed at myself. You forgot to turn on the camera.

I flipped a small switch on the camera. I pulled the cover away from the lens.

Just then Mr. Mortman's head turned toward me. Did he hear me?

I ducked down. Nothing happened. I stood up just a little and peeked in his office window.

No. He hadn't seen me.

CRUNCH. CRUNCH. Mr. Mortman was busy chewing. The sound of him chewing on the tarantula made me sick.

I forced myself to keep going. I stepped out from my hiding place behind the bookshelf. Then I looked through the camera lens again. I hoped Mr. Mortman wouldn't hear it when I pushed the button.

My finger pressed down gently. . . .

POP! There was a blinding light. I had forgotten about the flash!

"Who's there?" Mr. Mortman called out. He

whirled toward me. His huge, ugly eyes stared right at me.

Then he lunged out of his office — heading right for me!

"ARRGHH! You won't get away!" he yelled in his horrible monster's roar.

7

I turned and ran. I ran with my camera dangling from the strap over my arm. I ran for my life.

My feet slapped the tile floor loudly.

I could hear Mr. Mortman's leather shoes scuffling right behind me. I didn't dare turn around to see. I knew he was close.

"Come back here!" Mr. Mortman yelled.

I ran faster.

Please, I prayed. Just let me out of here!

"Keep running, little one," Mr. Mortman called. "I *love* fast food!"

Then he let out a terrible laugh.

I could see the front door. It was only inches away. I reached for it.

But something jerked me to a stop.

My camera strap was caught on one of the book carts!

Help! I wanted to yell. I yanked hard, trying to pull the camera loose.

The camera strap jerked free. But the camera clattered to the floor.

Oh, no. My picture. My proof! I thought. I can't leave the camera behind — can I?

I spun around to pick it up. Monster Mortman was right behind me. His tongue flicked out at me.

"You're just making me hungrier," he said. He reached for me. His huge eyes bobbled toward my face.

I couldn't move. I was frozen with fear. My legs felt thick and heavy.

The monster towered over me. His huge black mouth opened wide.

Then I smelled something sickening.

Yuk! Cricket breath!

And a small piece of tarantula leg stuck to the inside of his lip.

"My mouth is watering," Mr. Mortman

said. He moved closer to me, reaching for me. His mouth gaped open. "The spider was merely an appetizer," he said. "You're the MAIN COURSE!"

Fear pounded through me. Mr. Mortman was going to eat me alive!

For a minute, I just stood there. Frozen.

But then I snapped out of it.

NO! I thought. You won't get me that easily!

I ducked under Mr. Mortman's arm. He roared in anger. He tried to grab me and missed.

He roared again. Cricket breath!

I tried not to breathe in the smell. I just grabbed the camera and darted away. But Mr. Mortman was blocking my exit. I had no choice. I had to run deeper into the library . . . away from the front door!

"I've got you now!" Mr. Mortman yelled.

I dashed down an aisle. There was a long stretch of card catalogs. The monster was right behind me.

As I ran, I yanked open one of the card

catalog drawers. I left it sticking out in the aisle behind me.

Then I pulled open another drawer. And another. Maybe the drawers would slow him down and keep him away from me.

But Monster Mortman was fast. And powerful. He slammed the drawers shut, one by one. He gained on me and kept coming.

I reached the end of the aisle. There was nowhere else to go.

In a minute, he would have me trapped!

I opened the last drawer, pulling it with all my might. The drawer flew out of the cabinet. Cards spilled all over the floor.

"ARRGHHHH!" Mr. Mortman shouted furiously. His huge bobbling eyes stared at the mess. "My cards! My precious cards . . ."

I whirled around in terror. The monster was so close. All he had to do was grab me.

The monster leaned forward. But he didn't touch me. He started picking up the cards instead.

"My poor cards," he whined. "You messed them up."

One by one, he picked up the cards. He looked at each one carefully and tried to put them in order.

It was so crazy, I almost laughed. He was a monster — but he was a librarian, too! He had to clean everything up!

I was still shaking with fear. But I darted away from him and ran. Through the library. Out the door. Down the front steps.

I didn't stop running until I reached my house. Out of breath, I shoved my way through the front door.

At last! I was home safe. I slammed the door shut and took a deep breath.

Then I heard a voice behind me.

"I've got you now!" the voice boomed.

8

"Aaaahhhhh!" I screamed at the top of my lungs.

I whirled around, almost dropping my camera again. Someone was hiding behind the front door.

My little brother.

"Randy — you creep!" I cried.

Randy thought it was funny. He laughed so hard, he almost spit. "Did you think I was a monster?" he teased. "Or maybe scary Mr. Mortman?"

"Mr. Mortman *is* a monster," I told him. I held up my camera. "I've got proof!"

Who cares if you don't believe me? I

thought angrily. You'll see when the film is developed.

I turned away from Randy and stormed up to my room.

A few minutes later, Randy and my parents left. I was glad to be alone. I went downstairs and found our cordless phone. Then I went back to my room and called Aaron. Quickly I told him everything.

"I've got a picture to prove it!" I said.

"Of Mortman eating a tarantula?" Aaron asked.

"As a matter of fact, yes!" I almost shouted into the phone. So he'd know I was telling the truth.

"This I've got to see," Aaron said. I could tell from his voice that he still didn't believe me.

"Aaron," I said. "You're acting like a jerk. You're supposed to be my friend. You're supposed to believe me."

"Okay, okay," Aaron said. "Just tell me one thing. If Mortman's such a terrible monster, how did you get away?"

"I messed up the card catalog," I said. "You know how he hates to see those cards out of order. Maybe he didn't even see who I was. But I got the picture. I got my proof."

Aaron snickered. "Oh, right," he said with a laugh. "Your proof. But you're forgetting something, Lucy."

"What?" I asked.

"Your library card has your address on it," Aaron said. "Mortman knows where you live."

"So what?" I said.

"So Mortman could come to your house," Aaron said, teasing me. "He could be on his way right this minute!"

"That's not funny, Aaron," I said. But I started to feel jumpy. I walked over to the window and peeked out.

The front yard was empty.

But Aaron wouldn't stop. "If I were you, Lucy," he said, "I'd get out of there. Right now!"

He's right, I thought. Mr. Mortman might come after me. He does know my address!

I grabbed my camera.

"Lucy, I'm not kidding!" Aaron shouted into the phone. "Get out!"

I was still holding the cordless phone in one hand. In the other, I had my camera. I ran out of my room and down the stairs.

Aaron's right, I thought. *I'll be safer outside.*

I raced to the front door and yanked it open.

Mr. Mortman was standing right there in the doorway! And my parents weren't even home.

At least he had changed back to a normal-looking person. He wasn't a monster anymore.

Still, I was terrified.

"Aaaah!" I cried, letting out a little yell.

I dropped the cordless phone and lunged for the screen door. I locked it, locking Mr. Mortman outside.

"Good evening, Lucy," Mr. Mortman said in a pleasant voice. "May I come in for a minute?"

"No!" I shouted. "My parents aren't home!"

Mr. Mortman smiled.

Why did I tell him that? I yelled at myself.

"I mean, they'll be home any minute," I said quickly. "I mean they're in the bathroom." I turned toward the back of the house. "Mom?" I called. "Is Dad still cleaning his rifle?"

Maybe that will scare him away, I thought.

"That's okay," Mr. Mortman said. "I really came to see *you*, Lucy."

Uh-oh. That's what I was afraid of!

"You left your backpack at the library," Mr. Mortman said. "I brought it over."

I stared at the backpack and gulped.

What now? I thought. Does he really think I'm going to open the door?

"Uh, thanks," I said. "Could you just leave it on the doorstep, please?"

Mr. Mortman gave me a creepy smile again.

"Wouldn't it be easier if you opened the door?" he said. "Then I can hand it to you."

I just shook my head no.

"Okay," Mr. Mortman said. "I'll set it down right here."

43

He put my backpack on the front steps.

"Thank you," I said.

"No problem," Mr. Mortman answered. "It was on my way."

Then he turned and started down the walk. But he stopped when he was halfway. He turned around and stared at me.

"I'm looking forward to our next little chat at the library," he said.

I closed the door real fast. Then I watched him through the peephole in the door. Just in case he tried to come back or something.

When my parents got home, I ran out to the driveway. I had my camera with me. I grabbed my dad before he was out of the car.

"Dad! Mom! He was here!" I told them. "Mr. Mortman was here! We've got to get this film developed — now! I took a picture that proves he's a monster!"

My mom sighed. "Calm down, Lucy," she said.

"No!" I said. "I can't calm down. He followed me home!"

When I said that, my parents looked at each other. They looked worried.

"He followed you home? For no reason?" my dad said.

"Well, I forgot my backpack at the library," I explained. "He brought it over. He said it was on his way home."

"That was very nice of him," my mom said. "But Mr. Mortman lives all the way across town. It wasn't on his way at all."

"I knew it!" I shouted. "He's after me! Please, Dad? Can't we go to the photo store now? It's going to close."

My parents talked together for a minute. Finally they said yes. They would drive me to the photo store so I could drop off the film. Then we could all eat dinner at the mall.

After we ate, we went back to the photo store. I ran inside and paid for the pictures.

Now they'll see, I thought.

I know I'm not supposed to grab. But I grabbed the pictures from the clerk in the photo store.

The pictures fell out of my hands onto the ground.

"Now look what you've done!" I yelled at my little brother.

"Randy! Get in the car," my dad called.

Randy whined, but he went back to the car.

I bent down to pick up the photos.

But someone beat me to it. As I knelt, I saw a man's hand reach for the pictures, too.

"Here, let me help you," a voice said.

I froze. I *knew* that voice. It was Mr. Mortman!

9

I looked up slowly. My whole body was shaking.

"M-Mr. M-Mortman?" I said. "What are *you* doing here?"

Mr. Mortman smiled, but it was a mean smile. His beady black eyes stared hard at me. He clutched my photos in his slimy hands.

"Hello, Lucy," he said. I was still crouching on the ground. He towered over me.

"Why are you here?" I asked him again.

"I eat here at the mall almost every night," he said.

No, you don't, I wanted to scream. You're following me!

I slowly stood up.

"What's wrong, Lucy?" Mr. Mortman asked. "You look a little nervous. Thinking about monsters again?"

I gulped. He knows! I thought. He knows that I know he's a monster.

Before I could say anything, he opened his mouth just an inch. All of a sudden something popped out of his mouth. A tarantula leg!

I wanted to scream. I glanced over at my mom and dad. They hadn't seen it. They weren't even paying attention.

Was Mr. Mortman going to change into a monster right here in the parking lot?

When I looked back, Mr. Mortman was normal again. Then my dad turned around.

"Oh, Mr. Mortman," he said. "Thank you for bringing Lucy's backpack home today."

"No problem. It was on my way," Mr. Mortman insisted.

He's lying, I thought. I wanted to get away from him as fast as I could.

"Can we go now, Dad?" I said. I tugged on his arm. "We've got to *go*!"

"Then you'll want your pictures," Mr.

Mortman said. He handed them to me with another creepy smile.

I turned my back on Mr. Mortman in a rude way.

"Take it easy, Lucy," my dad said. He gave Mr. Mortman a look. It said, "Sorry. I don't know why Lucy's acting this way."

"Lucy has been in a strange mood recently," my mother explained.

Mr. Mortman nodded. "Yes. It's as if she has something on her mind," he said.

My mom's eyes darted to my dad's. They gave each other another one of those looks. As if they were still worried. Then my mom turned back to Mr. Mortman.

"Why don't you come to dinner tomorrow night?" my mother suddenly offered.

"Yes," my dad joined in. "Good idea! Lucy's been talking a lot about you. It would be nice to get to know you better."

I glared at my mother. I can't believe it! I thought. She's inviting the monster to come to our house!

"I'd love to," Mr. Mortman said. "Thank you.

It will be so nice to eat a home-cooked meal."

NO! Don't invite him! I wanted to shout. Don't let him come!

I waited until he was gone. Then I begged my mom and dad to listen. But they wouldn't change their minds. No matter what I said, they just told me, "Don't worry. We know what's best."

The next night, we waited for Mr. Mortman to arrive. I was so scared, I chewed on my fingernails. I only do that when I'm really worried.

I got out the picture of Mr. Mortman's office again. I decided to try one more time.

"Don't you see he's a monster?" I told my parents. "Please — just *look* at this picture. It proves it."

My mom and dad stared at the photo. It was just a picture of an empty office.

"He's not there," my mom said.

"I know," I said. "That's just it! He didn't show up in the picture — because he's a monster!"

My mom shook her head.

"I don't care if he turns into a drooling werewolf," she said. "He's coming to dinner tonight."

Finally the doorbell rang. My dad answered it and showed Mr. Mortman into the living room. My brother and I stood as far away from him as we could.

"What a lovely house," Mr. Mortman said, looking around. "This is so kind of you. I've been looking forward to this so much."

"We have, too," my mom said.

"Good evening, Lucy," Mr. Mortman said. "And so nice to see you again, young Randy. Will you be joining us for the Summer Reading program next year?"

"Uh, I don't know," Randy said. "Can I think about it?"

"Of course," Mr. Mortman said. He patted Randy on the head.

My mom pointed to a platter of tiny meatballs. Each one had a toothpick in it. "Lucy, offer Mr. Mortman a meatball," she said.

I held the platter. Mr. Mortman took a meatball and ate it.

"Ummm, delicious," he said. "What's for dinner?"

My mother glanced at my dad like they had a secret. "Well, it was going to be a surprise," my mom said.

"But since you asked —" my dad said, "*you* are."

Mr. Mortman's mouth fell open. "I'm sorry," he mumbled, "but I thought you said . . . "

My father nodded. "That's right," he said. "*You.* You're for dinner!"

All of a sudden, my mother's head started to change. It grew long and pointy. So did my dad's.

Their heads looked like snake heads! Only much bigger. And uglier, too. Scales popped out all over. Their skin turned green. Their eyes were huge, round, and cold.

My parents were monsters, too!

10

"No. Please. There must be some mistake. . . ." Mr. Mortman cried.

He crouched down in fear. He went lower and lower, trying to escape.

It was too late. By then my parents were much bigger than Mr. Mortman. They towered over him. They opened their jaws. I saw long, sharp fangs inside.

Then my parents closed in. I couldn't watch, so I looked away. So did my brother. But we saw the shadows on the wall.

CRACK. CRUNCH.

The noise was so loud, some of the furniture shook. The tray of meatballs rattled.

One meatball fell off and rolled across the floor.

Our dog jumped up and ate the meatball in one bite.

At the same time, my parents ate Mr. Mortman, bit by bit until he was gone.

When I looked at my parents again, they were wiping their mouths with napkins.

For a minute, I was so surprised I couldn't talk. Neither could Randy.

"Whoa!" I finally said.

"Oh, man!" Randy squeaked out.

Slowly, my parents changed back into human beings. Only their fangs were left.

"That was a close one," my dad admitted. "Now listen, both of you. You can never let anyone know we're monsters."

Randy and I nodded our heads. "We know that," we both said.

"Lucy, it won't be long before your training fangs grow in," my mother said. "And then Randy will get his, too."

"Wow!" I blurted out. "Really? We're also going to be monsters?"

"That's right," my mom said. "And guess what, Lucy? Pretty soon, you will be able to change shape. Just like Dad and I do."

"That's so cool!" Randy said.

"But remember — you can't tell anyone," my mom said.

"Do you know why?" my dad asked.

. I knew the answer right away. "People might be scared of us," I said. "And they might tell other people about us."

My mom nodded. "Most people don't like monsters. Except in stories."

I nodded. That was true.

"We can't allow any other monsters in town, either," my dad went on.

"Yeah," Randy agreed. "Other monsters might tell people about us. And if people found out, they would chase us away."

"Or worse," my dad said quietly.

My mom took a napkin and dabbed at something on my dad's lip.

"Mr. Mortman is the first monster we've seen in twenty years," my dad said.

"That's why we didn't believe you at first,

Lucy," my mom said. "But now he's gone. We'll be safe for a long time."

"Oh, no!" Randy said. He pointed out the window. "Another one!"

We all looked out the window.

A short monster was hurrying toward the front door. This one had ugly green and orange skin. And five fangs.

"What are we going to do?" I asked.

"We'd better let him in," my dad said.

I opened the door. My parents started to change shape again. My mom's head began growing long and pointy.

All at once, the short monster in the doorway pulled off his mask. It wasn't a monster. It was Aaron!

"Hey! What's up?" Aaron asked. He had a big grin.

I looked at my parents. They had already snapped back to normal.

"Oh, we just finished dinner," my dad said. He gave me a wink.

"Aw, man. Anything left?" Aaron asked.

"No," my dad said, hiding a smile.

"Well, what's for dessert?" Aaron asked.

We all stared at Aaron.

"Well, it was going to be a surprise," my mom said. "But since you asked . . ."

Oh, no, I thought. She's just kidding, isn't she?

"You like cherry pie?" my dad asked. He reached over to the table and picked up a pie.

"Sure!" Aaron said happily. "But first I want to see Lucy's monster picture."

"Oh, I don't have it," I told him.

"How come?" Aaron asked.

"Well . . ." I didn't know how to explain. So I looked at my parents.

"You'd never believe it," my father said finally.

"Why not?" Aaron asked.

"Well . . ." my mom started. But she didn't go on. She was stuck, too.

"Let's just say this. It's a hard story to swallow!" I joked.

And everyone laughed, except Aaron.